THE WOODLAND CHRISTMAS BALL

ANN BRADY

It was getting cold in the wood, and the Little Friends had started collecting leaves, grass, and food ready for the winter.

When the snow came, all the Little Friends would hide away until springtime.
And, because the friends wouldn't see each other for a long time, they had decided to have a big party called the Christmas Ball.

Everyone would get dressed in their best outfits and have some fun before settling down to sleep.

Sarah Butterfly loved the Christmas Ball because it meant she could show off the beautiful colours of her wings.

Sarah was very pretty and, when the sunlight shone, it made the colours of her wings glitter and sparkle.

There were lots of things to organise for the
Ball with everyone helping to get the clearing
ready. First, they swept away the dead leaves,
and then they polished the mushrooms.

Next, the Little Friends gathered lots of food,
as they wanted something nice to eat.
There would also be a place for dancing as the ants
were bringing their musical instruments to play.

No party would look right without some
decorations, so Sammy Spider was asked to weave
some cobwebs into the trees so
the glow-worms could hang on them,
taking turns to light up the party.

This year the Little Friends had invited some of
the other animals living in the wood.
Godfrey Grasshopper told Freddie Fly,
"Please go and ask Jenny Wren, Basil Blue Tit,
Timmy Tortoise, and Dora Dormouse
to come to the Ball."

Feeling very important with the job he had been

given, Freddie flew away over the treetops to look

for the Special Friends.

Seeing Jenny Wren gathering twigs, Freddie called out, "Jenny, would you like to come to the Christmas Ball?" Jenny Wren was a shy bird and didn't like being around lots of other creatures, but knowing how special it was to be invited to the Christmas Ball, she said, "I would love to come to the Ball. Thank you for inviting me."

And she flew away to get ready.

While he was flying, Freddie met Basil Blue Tit and asked,

"Would you like to come to the Woodland Christmas Ball?"

Basil smiled and said,

"Of course I'll come. Thank you."

And he flew away to make himself look nice.

Then, Freddie Fly saw Timmy Tortoise.

Timmy was quite excited at being invited, and he said,

"Thank you, but I had better start walking now as

it is a long way and I only move slowly.

But I will be there!"

Finally, Freddie met Dora Dormouse.

She was very happy to be invited and said,

"I can't wait for the Ball."

Then she set off up the pathway.

After Freddie had asked everyone, he flew back
to the woods to help with gathering the leaves
and flowers needed for their extra guests.

All day the Little Friends worked hard to make the
clearing look nice. Just as the sun went down and
the moon woke up, they all went home to get ready.

The first to arrive were the ants,
Annie, Abby, Alex and Andy, who set up their musical
instruments at the edge of the dance floor.

Annie played the flute, Abby the harp, Alex the trumpet, and
Andy the drums. Andy liked playing the drums because he
could bang them and make lots of noise.
The Ants could all sing as well and the Little Friends loved to
listen to them whenever they could.

Next to arrive was Flora Frog with Godfrey Grasshopper.
They had come early to check that everything was ready
and that the glow worms were going to light up the dance
floor. Their lights would make the place look very pretty.

Not long after, everyone else arrived, greeting each other
as if they hadn't seen them for days.

Finally, the Special Friends arrived.
Jenny Wren and Basil Blue Tit flew in together,
and even Timmy Tortoise arrived on time with
Dora Dormouse sitting on his back.

That just left Sarah Butterfly who was the last to arrive
because she wanted to make a big entrance. And she did,
looking lovely with her wings shining and sparkling in the
light from the moon and the glow worms.
All the Little Friends were amazed at
how pretty she looked.

Soon everyone was dancing
and chatting to each other.

The Ball lasted late into the night,
with everyone enjoying themselves so much.

But, all good things must end and finally, when they were all tired, Flora Frog said, "I think it's time for bed. We've all had a lovely party but now it's time to go to sleep. Goodnight everyone."

And calling,

"Merry Christmas,"

all the Little Friends, and their four
special guests, went home to settle down
for the winter.

As she flew home,
Sarah Butterfly felt very happy indeed.

The aim of the **Kids4Kids** is to promote children's books, especially those written by children.

Are you a writer of children's stories, or a young person who wants to try writing a story?

Visit: **www.kids4kids.org.uk**

Little Friends
Woodland Adventures Series

Bella's Birthday Surprise (2nd Edition: 9781912472000 / 9781912472017)
The Woodland Christmas Ball (2nd Edition: 9781912472109 / 9781912472116)
Timmy's New Friend (1st Edition: 9781912472086 / 9781912472093)
Playing Hide & Seek (1st Edition: 9781912472048 / 9781912472055)
Ouch! It Hurts (1st Edition: 9781912472062 / 9781912472079)
The Missing Ants (1st Edition: 9781912472024 / 9781912472031)

Published in the United Kingdom by Kids4Kids,
an imprint of Wordcatcher Publishing Group Ltd.

Category: Children's Picture Book / Age 3-5

Lightning Source UK Ltd.
Milton Keynes UK
UKHW052152291221
396365UK00002B/49